ISBN: 1-877719-42-0

Printed in Singapore

Precious ARE THE Promises

Edited by Paul C. Brownlow

Brownlow

Brownlow Publishing Company, Inc.

LITTLE TREASURES
MINIATURE BOOKS

CONTENTS

ABUNDANT LIVING

The thief comes only
to steal and kill and destroy;
I have come that they may have
life, and have it to the full.

JOHN 10:10

You will seek me and find me when
you seek me with all your heart.

JEREMIAH 29:13

Blessed are the peacemakers,
for they will be called sons of God.

MATTHEW 5:9

Without faith it is
impossible to please God.

HEBREWS 11:6

Above all else, guard your heart,
for it is the wellspring of life.

PROVERBS 4:23

Remember this:
Whoever sows sparingly
will also reap sparingly,
and whoever sows generously
will also reap generously.

2 CORINTHIANS 9:6

Trust in the Lord and do good;
dwell in the land and enjoy
safe pasture.

PSALM 37:3

Give, and it will be given to you.
A good measure, pressed down,
shaken together and running over,
will be poured into your lap.
For with the measure you use,
it will be measured to you.

LUKE 6:38

Commit to the Lord whatever you do,
and your plans will succeed.

PROVERBS 16:3

When a man's ways are pleasing
to the Lord, he makes even his
enemies live at peace with him.

PROVERBS 16:7

He is like a tree planted by streams
of water, which yields its fruit
in season and whose leaf does not
wither. Whatever he does prospers.

PSALM 1:3

The greatest among you will be your servant. For whoever exalts himself will be humbled, and whoever humbles himself will be exalted.

MATTHEW 23:11-12

God is able to make all grace abound to you, so that in all things at all times, having all that you need, you will abound in every good work.

2 CORINTHIANS 9:8

Whoever drinks the water
I give him will never thirst. Indeed,
the water I give him will become in
him a spring of water welling up
to everlasting life.

JOHN 4:14

Delight yourself in the Lord
and he will give you the
desires of your heart.

PSALM 37:4

But seek first his kingdom
and his righteousness,
and all these things will be
given to you as well.

MATTHEW 6:33

Cast your cares on the Lord
and he will sustain you; he will
never let the righteous fall.

PSALM 55:22

GOD CARES

Cast all your anxiety on him
because he cares for you.

1 PETER 5:7

Once you were not a people,
but now you are the people of God;
once you had not received mercy,
but now you have received mercy.

1 PETER 2:10

I will not forget you!
See, I have engraved you
on the palms of my hands.

Isaiah 49:15-16

But because of his great love for us,
God, who is rich in mercy, made us
alive with Christ even when we were
dead in transgressions—it is by grace
you have been saved.

Ephesians 2:4-5

For as high as the heavens
are above the earth, so great is his
love for those who fear him.

PSALM 103:11

The God of all comfort,
who comforts us in all our troubles,
so that we can comfort those
in any trouble.

2 CORINTHIANS 1:3-4

Because of the Lord's great love
we are not consumed, for his
compassions never fail.
They are new every morning;
great is your faithfulness.

LAMENTATIONS 3:22-23

As a father has compassion on his
children, so the Lord has compassion
on those who fear him.

PSALM 103:13

Not only so, but we also rejoice in our sufferings, because we know that suffering produces perseverance; perseverance, character; and character, hope. And hope does not disappoint us, because God has poured out his love into our hearts by the Holy Spirit, whom he has given us.

ROMANS 5:3-5

For where two or three
come together in my name,
there am I with them.

MATTHEW 18:20

He tends his flock like a shepherd:
He gathers the lambs in his arms and
carries them close to his heart; he
gently leads those that have young.

ISAIAH 40:11

Each man should give what he has
decided in his heart to give, not
reluctantly or under compulsion,
for God loves a cheerful giver.

2 CORINTHIANS 9:7

For the Lord loves the just
and will not forsake his faithful ones.
They will be protected forever.

PSALM 37:28

I will lie down and sleep in peace,
for you alone, O Lord, make me
dwell in safety.

PSALM 4:8

How great is the love the Father
has lavished on us, that we should
be called children of God!
And that is what we are!

1 JOHN 3:1

The Lord is righteous in all his ways
and loving toward all he has made.

PSALM 145:17

God is not unjust; he will not forget
your work and the love you have
shown him as you have helped
his people and continue
to help them.

HEBREWS 6:10

Consider the ravens:
They do not sow or reap,
they have no storeroom or barn;
yet God feeds them.
And how much more valuable
you are than birds!

LUKE 12:24

GOD IS FAITHFUL

He has given us his very great
and precious promises, so that
through them you may participate
in the divine nature and escape
the corruption in the world
caused by evil desires.

2 PETER 1:4

God is not a man, that he should lie, nor a son of man, that he should change his mind. Does he speak and then not act? Does he promise and not fulfill?

NUMBERS 23:19

If we are faithless, he will remain faithful, for he cannot disown himself.

2 TIMOTHY 2:13

The Lord is not slow
in keeping his promise,
as some understand slowness.
He is patient with you,
not wanting anyone to perish,
but everyone to come
to repentance.

2 PETER 3:9

I the Lord do not change.

MALACHI 3:6

Know therefore that the Lord your God is God; he is the faithful God, keeping his covenant of love to a thousand generations of those who love him and keep his commands.

DEUTERONOMY 7:9

Worship the Lord your God; it is he who will deliver you from the hand of all your enemies.

2 KINGS 17:39

Since we have these promises, dear friends, let us purify ourselves from everything that contaminates body and spirit, perfecting holiness out of reverence for God.

2 CORINTHIANS 7:1

The Lord is faithful to all his promises and loving toward all he has made.

PSALM 145:13

GOD OUR REFUGE

God is our refuge and strength,
an ever-present help in trouble.

PSALM 46:1

Oh, praise the greatness of our God!
He is the Rock, his works are perfect,
and all his ways are just. A faithful
God who does no wrong,
upright and just is he.

DEUTERONOMY 32:3-4

If you make the Most High your dwelling—even the Lord, who is my refuge—then no harm will befall you, no disaster will come near your tent.

PSALM 91:9-10

The Lord is my rock, my fortress and my deliverer; my God is my rock, in whom I take refuge.

2 SAMUEL 22:2-3

The eternal God is your refuge, and underneath are the everlasting arms.

DEUTERONOMY 33:27

He will cover you with his feathers, and under his wings you will find refuge.

PSALM 91:4

He who gives strength to the weary and increases the power of the weak.

ISAIAH 40:29

HEAVEN

I am coming soon. Hold on
to what you have, so that no one
will take your crown.

REVELATION 3:11

The Lord will rescue me from
every evil attack and will bring me
safely to his heavenly kingdom.
To him be glory for ever and ever.

2 TIMOTHY 4:18

The world and its desires pass away,
but the man who does the will of God
lives forever.

1 JOHN 2:17

Here is a trustworthy saying:
If we died with him, we will also live
with him; if we endure, we will also
reign with him. If we disown him,
he will also disown us.

2 TIMOTHY 2:11-12

We fix our eyes not on what is seen, but on what is unseen. For what is seen is temporary, but what is unseen is eternal.

2 CORINTHIANS 4:18

Whoever puts his faith in the Son has eternal life, but whoever rejects the Son will not see that life, for God's wrath remains on him.

JOHN 3:36

The dead in Christ will rise first.
After that, we who are still alive
and are left will be caught up
with them in the clouds
to meet the Lord in the air.
And so we will be with
the Lord forever.

1 THESSALONIANS 4:16-17

I am the resurrection and the life.
He who believes in me will live,
even though he dies; and whoever
lives and believes in me
will never die.

JOHN 11:25-26

He will swallow up death forever.
The Sovereign Lord will wipe away
the tears from all faces.

ISAIAH 25:8

We believe that Jesus died and
rose again and so we believe
that God will bring with Jesus
those who sleep in him.

1 THESSALONIANS 4:14

I write these things to you who
believe in the name of the Son of God
so that you may know that you
have eternal life.

1 JOHN 5:13

Christ was sacrificed once to take away the sins of many people; and he will appear a second time, not to bear sin, but to bring salvation to those who are waiting for him.

HEBREWS 9:28

Now we know that if the earthly tent we live in is destroyed, we have a building from God, an eternal house in heaven, not built by human hands.

2 CORINTHIANS 5:1

41

In his great mercy
he has given us new birth
into a living hope through
the resurrection of
Jesus Christ from the dead,
and into an inheritance
that can never perish,
spoil or fade—
kept in heaven for you.

1 PETER 1:3-4

Christ is the mediator of a new
covenant, that those who are called
may receive the promised
eternal inheritance.

HEBREWS 9:15

But our citizenship is in heaven.
And we eagerly await
a Savior from there,
the Lord Jesus Christ.

PHILIPPIANS 3:20-21

Sell your possessions and give
to the poor. Provide purses for
yourselves that will not wear out,
a treasure in heaven that will
not be exhausted, where no thief
comes near and no moth destroys.
For where your treasure is,
there your heart will be also.

LUKE 12:33-34

Not everyone who says to me, "Lord, Lord," will enter the kingdom of heaven, but only he who does the will of my Father who is in heaven.

MATTHEW 7:21

We know that when he appears, we shall be like him, for we shall see him as he is.

1 JOHN 3:2

HOLY LIVING

Make every effort to live in peace with all men and to be holy; without holiness no one will see the Lord.

HEBREWS 12:14

Blessed are those who are persecuted because of righteousness, for theirs is the kingdom of heaven.

MATTHEW 5:10

For we are God's workmanship, created in Christ Jesus to do good works, which God prepared in advance for us to do.

EPHESIANS 2:10

Humble yourselves, therefore, under God's mighty hand, that he may lift you up in due time.

1 PETER 5:6

Therefore we do not lose heart.
Though outwardly we are wasting
away, yet inwardly we are being
renewed day by day.

2 CORINTHIANS 4:16

I am the bread of life.
He who comes to me will never go
hungry, and he who believes in me
will never be thirsty.

JOHN 6:35

His divine power has given us
everything we need for life and
godliness through our knowledge
of him who called us by his
own glory and goodness.

2 PETER 1:3

Do not be afraid, little flock,
for your Father has been pleased
to give you the kingdom.

LUKE 12:32

49

Trust in the Lord with all your heart
and lean not on your own understanding; in all your ways acknowledge him,
and he will make your paths straight.

PROVERBS 3:5-6

If we confess our sins,
he is faithful and just and will
forgive us our sins and purify us
from all unrighteousness.

1 JOHN 1:9

Therefore, since we have been justified through faith, we have peace with God through our Lord Jesus Christ.

ROMANS 5:1

And we know that in all things God works for the good of those who love him, who have been called according to his purpose.

ROMANS 8:28

Whoever humbles himself like
this child is the greatest in the
kingdom of heaven.

MATTHEW 18:4

Consider it pure joy, my brothers,
whenever you face trials of
many kinds, because you know
that the testing of your faith
develops perseverance.

JAMES 1:2-3

It is for your good that I am going away. Unless I go away, the Counselor will not come to you; but if I go, I will send him to you.

JOHN 16:7

Let us not become weary in doing good, for at the proper time we will reap a harvest if we do not give up.

GALATIANS 6:9

But when he, the Spirit of truth, comes, he will guide you into all truth. He will not speak on his own; he will speak only what he hears, and he will tell you what is yet to come.

JOHN 16:13

Do not judge, and you will not be judged. Do not condemn, and you will not be condemned. Forgive, and you will be forgiven.

LUKE 6:37

For God did not call us to be impure,
but to live a holy life. Therefore,
he who rejects this instruction
does not reject man but God,
who gives you his Holy Spirit.

I THESSALONIANS 4:7-8

Since everything will be destroyed in this way, what kind of people ought you to be? You ought to live holy and godly lives as you look forward to the day of God and speed its coming. That day will bring about the destruction of the heavens by fire, and the elements will melt in the heat.

2 PETER 3:11-12

JESUS CHRIST

The Word became flesh and
made his dwelling among us.
We have seen his glory,
the glory of the One and Only,
who came from the Father,
full of grace and truth.

JOHN 1:14

The Son is the radiance of God's glory
and the exact representation of
his being, sustaining all things
by his powerful word.

HEBREWS 1:3

Come to me, all you
who are weary and burdened,
and I will give you rest.

MATTHEW 11:28

But now in Christ Jesus you who
once were far away have been
brought near through the
blood of Christ.

EPHESIANS 2:13

But God demonstrates his own love
for us in this: While we were still
sinners, Christ died for us.

ROMANS 5:8

I write to you, dear children, because your sins have been forgiven on account of his name.

1 JOHN 2:12

For you know the grace of our Lord Jesus Christ, that though he was rich, yet for your sakes he became poor, so that you through his poverty might become rich.

2 CORINTHIANS 8:9

He who did not spare his own Son,
but gave him up for us all—how
will he not also, along with him,
graciously give us all things.

ROMANS 8:32

But thanks be to God!
He gives us the victory through
our Lord Jesus Christ.

1 CORINTHIANS 15:57

He who has the Son has life;
he who does not have the
Son of God does not have life.

1 JOHN 5:12

But thanks be to God, who always
leads us in triumphal procession in
Christ and through us spreads
everywhere the fragrance of
the knowledge of him.

2 CORINTHIANS 2:14-15

I have come into the world
as a light, so that no one
who believes in me
should stay in darkness.

JOHN 12:46

I can do everything through him
who gives me strength.

PHILIPPIANS 4:13

Salvation is found in no one else;
for there is no other name under
heaven given to me by which
we must be saved.

ACTS 4:12

Therefore he is able to save
completely those who come to God
through him, because he always
lives to intercede for them.

HEBREWS 7:25

And my God will meet all your needs according to his glorious riches in Christ Jesus.

PHILIPPIANS 4:19

In him and through faith in him we may approach God with freedom and confidence.

EPHESIANS 3:12

Jesus Christ is the same yesterday
and today and forever.

HEBREWS 13:8

I am the good shepherd.
The good shepherd lays down
his life for the sheep.

JOHN 10:11

NEVER FORSAKEN

Fear not, for I have redeemed you;
I have summoned you by name;
you are mine.

ISAIAH 43:1

Those who know your name will trust
in you, for you, Lord, have never
forsaken those who seek you.

PSALM 9:10

I will put my law in their minds and write it on their hearts. I will be their God and they will be my people.

JEREMIAH 31:33

Submit yourselves, then to God. Resist the devil, and he will flee from you. Come near to God and he will come near to you.

JAMES 4:7-8

What is man that you are mindful of him, the son of man that you care for him? You made him a little lower than the heavenly beings and crowned him with glory and honor.

PSALM 8:4-5

Keep your lives free from the love of money and be content with what you have, because God has said, "Never will I leave you; never will I forsake you."

HEBREWS 13:5

Know that the Lord is God. It is he
who made us, and we are his.

PSALM 100:3

But you are a chosen people,
a royal priesthood, a holy nation,
a people belonging to God,
that you may declare the praises of
him who called you out of darkness
into his wonderful light.

1 PETER 2:9

POWER OF GOD

Praise be to the Lord,
to God our Savior, who daily
bears our burdens.

PSALM 68:19

Surely the arm of the Lord
is not too short to save,
nor his ear too dull to hear.

ISAIAH 59:1

Because he himself suffered when he was tempted, he is able to help those who are being tempted.

HEBREWS 2:18

I am the Lord, the God of all mankind. Is anything too hard for me?

JEREMIAH 32:27

My soul finds rest in God alone; my salvation comes from him.

PSALM 62:1

And if the Spirit of him who raised
Jesus from the dead is living in you,
he who raised Christ from the dead
will also give life to your mortal
bodies through his Spirit,
who lives in you.

ROMANS 8:11

I have swept away your offenses
like a cloud, your sins like the
morning mist. Return to me,
for I have redeemed you.

ISAIAH 44:22

73

My flesh and my heart may fail,
but God is the strength of my heart
and my portion forever.

PSALM 73:26

God is faithful; he will not
let you be tempted beyond what you
can bear. But when you are tempted,
he will also provide a way out so that
you can stand up under it.

1 CORINTHIANS 10:13

For the Lord your God
is the one who goes with you
to fight for you against your
enemies to give you victory.

Deuteronomy 20:4

Great is our Lord
and mighty in power;
his understanding
has no limit.

Psalm 147:5

Neither death nor life,
neither angels nor demons,
neither the present nor the future,
nor any powers, neither height nor
depth, nor anything else in all
creation, will be able to separate
us from the love of God that is in
Christ Jesus our Lord.

ROMANS 8:38-39

Though I walk in the midst of trouble, you preserve my life; you stretch out your hand against the anger of my foes, with your right hand you save me.

PSALM 138:7

"Don't be afraid," the prophet answered. "Those who are with us are more than those who are with them."

2 KINGS 6:16

I have told you these things, so that in me you may have peace. In this world you will have trouble. But take heart! I have overcome the world.

JOHN 16:33

For the Lord God is a sun and shield; the Lord bestows favor and honor. No good thing does he withhold from those whose walk is blameless.

PSALM 84:11

The Lord gives sight to
the blind, the Lord lifts up those
who are bowed down, the Lord
loves the righteous.

PSALM 146:8

So we say with confidence,
"The Lord is my helper; I will not be
afraid. What can man do to me?"

HEBREWS 13:6

I lift up my eyes to the hills—
where does my help come from?
My help comes from the Lord, the
Maker of heaven and earth.

PSALM 121:1-2

The Lord reigns, let the earth be glad;
let the distant shores rejoice.

PSALM 97:1

PRAYER

Ask and it will be given
to you; seek and you will find;
knock and the door will be
opened to you. For everyone who
asks receives; he who seeks finds;
and to him who knocks,
the door will be opened.

MATTHEW 7:7-8

We can have confidence
before God and receive from
him anything we ask, because
we obey his commands and
do what pleases him.

1 JOHN 3:21,22

Love your enemies and pray for those
that persecute you, that you may be
sons of your Father in heaven.

MATTHEW 5:44-45

If my people
who are called by my
name, will humble themselves
and pray and seek my face
and turn from their wicked ways,
then will I hear from heaven
and will forgive their sin
and will heal their land.

2 CHRONICLES 7:14

The eyes of the Lord are on
the righteous and his ears are
attentive to their cry.

PSALM 34:15

This is the confidence
we have in approaching God:
that if we ask anything according
to his will, he hears us.

1 JOHN 5:14

If you believe,
you will receive whatever
you ask for in prayer.

MATTHEW 21:22

I call to the Lord,
who is worthy of praise,
and I am saved from
my enemies.

2 SAMUEL 22:4

When you pray,
go into your room,
close the door and pray to
your Father, who is unseen.
Then your Father, who sees
what is done in secret
will reward you.

MATTHEW 6:6

Do not be anxious about anything, but in everything, by prayer and petition, with thanksgiving, present your requests to God. And the peace of God, which transcends all understanding, will guard your hearts and minds in Christ Jesus.

PHILIPPIANS 4:6-7

STRENGTH FOR TODAY

Even youths grow tired and weary,
and young men stumble and fall;
but those who hope in the Lord
will renew their strength.
They will soar on wings like eagles;
they will run and not grow weary,
they will walk and not be faint.

ISAIAH 40:30-31

For Christ's sake, I delight in
weaknesses, in insults, in hardships,
in persecutions, in difficulties.
For when I am weak,
then I am strong.

2 CORINTHIANS 12:10

It is God who arms me with strength
and makes my way perfect. You give
me your shield of victory; you stoop
down to make me great.

2 SAMUEL 22:33-36

Now to him who is able
to do immeasurably more than
all we ask or imagine, according to
his power that is at work within us,
to him be glory in the church and
in Christ Jesus throughout all
generations, for ever and ever!

EPHESIANS 3:20-21

For I command you today
to love the Lord your God,
to walk in his ways, and to keep
his commands, decrees and laws;
then you will live and increase,
and the Lord your God
will bless you.

DEUTERONOMY 30:16

WORD OF GOD

Heaven and earth will pass away,
but my words will never pass away.

MATTHEW 24:35

For you have been born again,
not of perishable seed, but imperishable, through the living and
enduring word of God.

1 PETER 1:23

The law of the Lord is perfect, reviving the soul. The statutes of the Lord are trustworthy, making wise the simple.

PSALM 19:7

The word of God is living and active. Sharper than any double-edged sword, it penetrates even to dividing soul and spirit, joints and marrow; it judges the thoughts and attitudes of the heart.

HEBREWS 4:12

"For my thoughts
are not your thoughts,
neither are your ways my ways,"
declares the Lord.
"As the heavens are higher
than the earth so are my ways
higher than your ways
and my thoughts than
your thoughts."

ISAIAH 55:8-9